NOAH
ILA'S STORY

NOAH
ILA'S STORY

A NOVEL BY SUSAN KORMAN

BASED ON THE SCREENPLAY WRITTEN BY
DARREN ARONOFSKY & ARI HANDEL

TITAN BOOKS

Noah: Ila's Story
Print edition ISBN: 9781783292585
E-book edition ISBN: 9781783292592

Published by Titan Books
A division of Titan Publishing Group Ltd
144 Southwark St, London SE1 0UP

First edition: March 2014
1 3 5 7 9 10 8 6 4 2

Printed and bound in the United Kingdom..

TITAN BOOKS.COM

NOAH
ILA'S STORY

1

THE YOUNG GIRL MOANED, HER EYES FLITTING OPEN. A deep gash had pierced her belly, and blood was soaking through her dress.

Ila tried to sit up, but it hurt too much. She had no idea how long she'd been lying here, alone in the dark and cold. Right now the camp was silent and still. But earlier it had been filled with sounds, loud, terrifying sounds...

First hoofbeats and loud cries from a band of raiders. Then desperate screams from her mother and her aunts. The men in Ila's family had tried to fight back, but the raiders had arrived so swiftly, and with no warning... Even Ila and the other children had quickly seen that there was almost no chance of overpowering them.

"Mother," Ila whimpered now. But she knew her mother was dead. A brutal raider, his eyes gleaming like a snake's, had grabbed Mother. When she'd tried to fight, he had swiftly stabbed her with his spear.

Perhaps Father will find me, Ila thought. Father had rushed back into their tent for a weapon. He was very strong—able to lift Ila in his arms as easily as he lifted a sheaf of wheat. Surely he had managed to protect himself. Did he know she was here, wedged between wagons, wounded?

"Father?" she called. Pain tore through her as she made herself lift her head to look around.

Small fires smoldered around the camp, scattering embers into the air. The dim light was enough for her to see the ruins of their settlement—the blackened and burned-out wagons, a smashed urn, scraps of clothing, grain spilled across the ground.

A sharp wind blew, blowing dry dust everywhere. Ila tried to lift an arm to shield her eyes. When she dropped her arm again, she saw something else close by—bodies, a stack of lifeless bodies.

My family.

With a moan, she let her head fall back again. Her teeth chattered and her body trembled violently.

There's no one left but me, Ila realized. *I am the only one.*

She closed her eyes, and soon the thick blackness fell over her again like a blanket.

* * *

Ila drifted in and out of sleep, too weak to move or think about getting up.

"Do you think they're dead?" a voice asked suddenly.

Is that a boy? Ila wondered. She struggled to open her eyes.

"It looks that way," someone else answered.

A woman was speaking now. "It looks to me like they were gleaners. They must have been scavenging around here when raiders came."

"And someone scavenged from them," a man put in grimly. "There's nothing left here."

Ila moaned in pain.

"Shh," someone said. It was the boy again. "Father!" he cried. "I heard someone!"

"I heard someone too, Shem," answered the man. Ila thought she heard him moving nearby, perhaps he was looking around. "It doesn't seem possible, but maybe there is a survivor among these ruins."

Ila heard more footsteps. *Maybe they will find me.* Her eyes fluttered closed again. She was so tired... There was so much blood around her.

At last the boy stepped closer to where she lay. "Here, Father!" he yelled. "I found her. It's a girl!"

A woman carrying an infant hurried to Ila's side, murmuring soothing words. "It's all right... you'll be all right..."

Ila opened her eyes and looked up, blinking. Was that her mother? *No,* she remembered with a stab of pain. *My mother is gone.*

"What happened?" the woman was asking her. "Tell me what happened to you and your family."

She handed the infant to a younger boy. Now Ila could see the man—he was tall, with broad shoulders and a dark beard.

Ila's eyes closed again. Her throat felt dry and her eyes stung from the wind and all her tears. "Raiders... " she whispered. "Mother and Father and—"

"Never mind." The woman stroked Ila's hair and hushed her. "Rest now. You can tell us your story later. May I look at your wound?"

Ila stared up at the woman's face. She had kind, green eyes and dark hair. Her voice was soft and gentle. Ila nodded, letting the woman examine the bloody gash across her abdomen.

"It looks very deep," the woman murmured. "I'm going to try to bandage it now." She looked at Ila. "It's going to hurt. A lot," she added.

Ila nodded, grimacing as the woman swiped at the cut with some water.

"What's your name?" asked the woman.

"Ila. My name is Ila," she answered.

"Ila," the woman repeated with a smile. "My name is Naameh." She gestured to the older boy who had found Ila. "This is Shem. While I bandage your wound, he's going to hold your hand tight and he won't let go."

The boy named Shem took her hand. Just as Naameh had promised, he held it tightly while his mother nursed Ila's wound.

Ila looked away, grimacing in pain. Tears filled her eyes. *Mother, Father*, she thought.

Shem tightened his grip on her hand. "You are very brave," he told her solemnly. "Braver than I am, I think."

"You are braver than me too!" chimed in the younger boy. Ila thought his name was Ham.

She tried to smile her thanks. She held on tightly, closing her eyes again and letting herself doze.

Soon she heard more voices. This time they all belonged to men. There were some harsh shouts, followed by a flurry of commands.

Oh no. Ila's heart skipped a beat. Were the raiders back?

Naameh looked up, worried. "Do you see anyone, Noah?"

"Yes. A raiding party," he answered grimly. "They've seen us. We have to go."

"Now?" Naameh started to say. "But—"

"Yes, over the hill!" he commanded. "Run!"

Naameh grabbed the baby, and the next thing Ila knew, the man named Noah swooped down and gently lifted her off the ground.

The family ran from the raiders for a long time. Naameh and the boys seemed exhausted. Ila tried not to cry out from pain as she bounced along in Noah's arms.

At the bottom of the hill, the land looked burnt and scarred-looking. Ahead Ila could see clumps of skeletons hanging from tall spikes. She squinted. Were those spooky things real? She shivered and closed her eyes.

Naameh was staring at the dark, pitted landscape ahead. "No, Noah. No. We can't go there. It's the Watchers' Land."

Noah had stopped too, still holding Ila tightly. "The raiding party is right behind us, Naameh," she heard him say. He glanced over his shoulder again. "They've crested the ridge," he said. "We have no choice. Hurry!"

Naameh and her sons followed Noah across the border. Behind them, most of the raiders halted. But Ila heard Noah curse under his breath. A few of the raiders rushed after them.

Ila dozed again. She woke with a groan as Noah suddenly thrust her into Shem's arms.

Shem took her, his eyes on his father.

"Protect your mother first and last," he commanded the boy. "Now run. I love you!" He pulled out his knife and whirled toward the raiders.

The wound in Ila's belly throbbed as Shem raced away from Noah. Naameh hurried after them with Ham and the baby.

Ila closed her eyes. *Will Noah be safe?* she wanted to ask Shem. But she was too tired. Everything hurt so much...

When Ila woke, she could see that she and the others were in a deep crater. Peering down at them were about thirty giant creatures—they looked like they were made of stone or mud.

Impaled on pikes all around the rim of the crater were more of those spooky-looking skeletons.

Ila's head felt hot and her eyes burned. Scared, she turned to Shem, who was sitting nearby. "I must be dreaming," she murmured. "I see stone giants up there."

"Those creatures are Watchers," Shem whispered back.

"Watchers?" she echoed. "Are we in danger?"

"I am not sure. They captured Father and then they found us and trapped us all here." He looked at her as she winced. "Are you in a lot of pain?"

Ila wanted to be brave, but she was in pain. "It hurts a lot," she blurted out.

"Well, we think you are very strong," he said. "You do not have to talk, you know," he added. "Mother said that you are to save your strength."

Ila nodded. It hurt when she spoke, but she wanted to keep talking. She didn't want to think about her parents and the rest of her family right now.

While Shem stared at the Watchers, she stole another glance at him. She guessed he was about nine or ten, maybe a year older than she was.

He's very kind for a boy, she thought. Not like most of her boy cousins who teased her and rarely included her in their games and races.

"How did your family find me?" she asked.

"Uh..." Shem cast a quick look at his father. "We were traveling, on our way to see Grandfather. My father... Noah...

13

He has dreams—terrible dreams about the world ending and millions and millions of people dying in a massive flood. He says..." Shem swallowed, looking worried. "He says that he dreams of the Creator destroying the whole world."

"The whole world...?" Ila echoed. She could not imagine that—especially since her world had already been destroyed. Was Shem saying there was more destruction and violence to come?

"Father also dreamed of Grandfather's mountain," Shem went on. "Methuselah is the oldest man on earth. He has walked the land since Adam lived and is very wise. Father wants to see if he is still alive. He is very anxious to talk with Grandfather to—"

One of the Watchers started shouting again. Ila looked up to see that he was grizzled and covered with scars.

"That one is their leader," Shem whispered to her. "Samyaza."

"That's an abomination, Og!" Samyaza snapped at another one. "You should have killed them. They are trespassers and they must die!"

"We are here to see Methuselah—my grandfather," Noah called loudly.

Og looked toward the leader. "That man is a child of the old one, Samyaza!" he said. "That's why their lives were spared."

Samyaza scowled in anger. "Those are lies, Og. That's a man and nothing more!"

"But Samyaza..." Og tried to argue again.

"Do you forget how they betrayed the Creator?" Samyaza cut him off. "How mankind—"

"It is He who sends us," Noah yelled to them. "The Creator himself!"

Ila heard a few Watchers gasp.

"The Creator sent them?" one murmured.

"More lies," Samyaza snarled. "Leave them here to rot!"

Soon the Watchers marched away from the crater.

Shem looked worried again. "You should rest now," he said to Ila. "Don't worry. Father will think of something."

In the darkness, Ila tossed and turned. She was burning up and her face felt slick with sweat. Everything around her looked hazy, shimmering with a strange fog.

"Shem...?" she murmured. But he was no longer sitting there. Someone else, a tall figure with a dark beard, sat nearby now, watching her.

"Sleep," the man said gently. "You need to sleep."

"Father?" Ila blinked and stared up at him. His face looked so different... so far away. "Please sing to me," she murmured. "I want my daddy to sing to me."

"Hush, little one." The man reached out to stroke her hair. "The fever is making you see things. There's a song that my father used to sing to me when I could not sleep. Would you like me to sing it to you?"

Ila nodded yes. Was this man her father? she wondered. She still could not tell. Or maybe this was Shem's father, the man named Noah...?

She heard him start to sing softly.

> *The moon is high*
> *The trees entwined*
> *Your father waits for thee.*
> *To wrap you in his sheltering wings*
> *And whisper you to sleep.*
> *To wrap you in his welcome arms*
> *Until the night sky breaks*
> *Your father is*
> *The healing wind that whispers*
> *You to sleep*
> *That whispers as you sleep.*

The man rocked Ila back and forth.

He's not my daddy... Ila knew that now. The man was Shem's father.

"I am also an orphan, little Ila," Noah whispered. "I lost my father, too, when I was a child."

Ila closed her eyes again. The man wasn't singing any longer... Now he was quiet like her. His eyes were closed.

Maybe he's dreaming too, thought Ila.

* * *

Noah stood before his father at the ancient shrine. He had just turned thirteen—he was almost a man now. His father was blessing him.

"And so down to us the blessing passed... to my father, Methuselah and then to me... today that birthright passes to you, Noah, my son," Lamech said.

Noah's father took out a wooden box and carefully removed a holy talisman, a long snakeskin. He began to wrap it around himself.

"The Creator made Adam in his own image, and then placed the world in his care. This is the path we follow, Noah. This is your work now, your responsibility."

Noah watched as the holy talisman began to spread up Lamech's arm. It shimmered as Lamech spoke, glowing with a heavenly light.

"May you walk alongside the Creator in righteousness."

Noah stared in awe as Lamech stretched out his wrapped hand, holding his index finger close to Noah's finger. The talisman flickered and then began to crawl onto Noah's hand. His father gave him a reassuring nod. "So I say to you—"

Loud sounds and cries erupted, cutting off Lamech. Noah's father quickly yanked his wrapped hand away. "Men are coming! Hide, Noah! Now!"

Noah quickly ducked behind a rock. He peered past a stone, spying a group of miners who were guarded by fierce warlords clad in iron. In the distance, he could see the city. Smoke billowed from the spires of its tall **rough-hewn metal** buildings.

A *brutal and powerful-looking man stepped toward Lamech. It was Tubal-cain. He jammed a giant auger into the ground and removed a whitish-yellow stone.*

"Pure tzohar!" he declared.

Lamech marched toward the intruder. "This is the Creator's land. What are you doing?" he demanded.

In response, Tubal-cain backhanded Lamech hard across the face. Lamech tumbled backward into the dirt.

"The Creator?" Tubal-cain thundered. "My mines run dry. My city withers and must be fed. And what has He done? He cursed us to struggle by the sweat of our brows to survive. Damned if I don't do everything it takes to do just that—survive!"

Tubal-cain's eyes suddenly landed on the snakeskin talisman, still glimmering on Lamech's arm.

Noah heard him draw in a breath. "Damned if I don't take what I want!" he declared loudly. Then he pulled the shimmering reptile skin from Lamech's body. The holy talisman instantly lost its energy. Now it merely looked like dead skin.

Tubal-cain triumphantly tossed the skin around his shoulders, as though he had won it as a prize. "This relic belongs to Cain's line now!" he gloated. "The line of Seth ends here."

Noah gasped as Tubal-cain suddenly pulled out an axe and swung it hard at Lamech.

"Father!" Noah whispered. "Oh no... Father!"

Tubal-cain turned to his miners and gestured at the ground. "The land is ours. Now dig!"

Stunned, Noah raced out of the back of the ancient temple, tears streaming down his face. His kind, beloved father was gone forever.

Sometime later, Ila stirred. Soft voices whirled around her, but she didn't know whose they were. Her eyes felt too thick, too heavy, to open.

Now someone was looking at her bandages. Ila moaned in pain. Was it Naameh...? Ila was so tired... so hot...

Naameh gently unwound the bandages to check the young girl's wound. Noah watched his wife work.

"It's an ugly one," she murmured to Noah. "But if the fever doesn't take her, I think she will live.

"But..." Naameh drew in a breath. "She is barren now. This girl will never have children."

2

NEAR DAWN, ILA FELT HERSELF BEING LIFTED INTO NOAH'S arms again. Whispering to one another, the family hurried after the Watcher named Og through a dark desert.

Ila was tired, but she felt better. Naameh had felt her forehead and said it was cooler now; perhaps Ila's fever had broken.

The boys had to rush to keep up with the giant's huge strides and so did Naameh, carrying baby Japheth.

"Why are you helping us?" Ham asked the Watcher.

"For many reasons," Og explained as they moved along. "The Creator formed us on the second day, the day he made the heavens. We watched over the first humans, Adam and Eve, saw their love and also their frailty. When we saw their fall, we pitied them. So we glided through the clouds, down to earth. We were not made of stone then, but of light.

"It was not our place to help or interfere with humankind. It was our choice. And for that the Creator punished us. We turned to stone and became bound to your world. Still, we taught humankind all we knew of Creation.

"With our help, people rose from the dust. But then they turned our gifts into violence and destruction. When we were chased into this dark land, only one man protected us." He looked at Noah. "That was Methuselah."

Ila remembered Shem saying this name... Was that the name of Noah's grandfather?

"Most of us were killed—hunted for the light within us, known as tzohar," Og went on. "We begged the Creator to take us back into heaven, but He stayed silent. And now..."

Noah shifted Ila in his arms as the giant went on.

"And now, you, Noah, claim to have heard His call. Our leader, Samyaza, cannot accept this. How could the Creator call to a man, when it is men who have broken this world?" Og's voice softened. "But I look at you, Noah, and I see a glimmer of Adam—the man I knew, the man I came to help."

Ila dozed as they walked further along. At last they came to the foot of a mountain. It was green, rising above the empty dark plain. Ila thought she could see a few caves at the very top.

Noah set her down on a soft spot on the ground and then helped Naameh set up their camp.

"Shem and I will go alone to see Methuselah," Noah informed the others. "The rest of you will stay here until we return."

Ham's face fell. "Why can't I go too, Father?" he asked.

Noah kneeled to talk to him. "I need you to look after Mother."

Ham still looked disappointed. But obediently, he nodded. "I will, Father."

Naameh kissed Shem goodbye and then tapped him playfully on the nose. "And you look after Father!" she said teasingly.

They waved goodbye and started toward the mountain. As they passed Og, Ila saw Noah lean in to speak to the Watcher. "Will you watch over my family?" she heard him ask.

The giant nodded and spread out his arms. Now Ila could see that the strange-looking Watcher had not two, but six stony arms!

"Yes," Og answered with a faint smile. "They are in good hands."

While Shem and Noah were on the mountain, Ila rested. Naameh brought her some food and water, and checked her wound from time to time.

"You are healing, little one," Naameh said soothingly. "Soon you will be much stronger."

Without Shem there for company, Ila played with Ham

for a while. They took turns telling stories to one another and building towers out of rocks and sticks.

Later, Ila tried to nap again. Nearby, inside the tent, Naameh was nursing the baby.

Ila watched Naameh hold the tiny bundle close to her.

Mother. Father.

Grief cut through her, and Ila could not hold back her tears any longer. She could not believe they were gone.

Her family had always been working, wandering the land in search of food and grain and shelter. It was not an easy life.

But her parents had taught her to be strong.

There is too much to do for us to dwell on what is hard, her father always told her. *Fill your mind with what is good, Ila, the things you love.*

She rolled over and closed her eyes. She could easily picture Father's dancing eyes and his strong arms... how his beard tickled her when he lifted her up to his face.

And Mother... her quick smile and easy laugh. She sang so sweetly to Ila and was patient when she taught her how to stitch clothing and gather food.

Now she knew what Father had meant.

These are good memories, Ila thought. *I will keep my mind full of them.*

Soon she rolled over to look at Naameh and the baby again. Japheth was very tiny, with dark eyes and wisps of hair. Ila liked to watch him kick his legs.

Naameh saw her watching and flashed Ila a smile.

Ila smiled back. *As Naameh says, someday I will be strong again,* she thought.

And perhaps then she could find ways to pay back this loving family who had rescued her.

"Father!" Ham had been playing with Og for a few hours, darting in and out of the giant's legs, when he spotted Noah and Shem approaching the camp. Ham ran to Noah and hugged him.

Ila sat up. She felt relieved to see the two of them back safely from Methuselah's mountain.

"We have much to talk of," Noah began. "Let us eat and rest first and then we will tell you about Grandfather." He gave Ila a smile. "Our new daughter looks well rested and healthier. Naameh, you are a skillful nurse."

Later inside the tent, Ila waited for Noah and Naameh with Shem and Ham. Shem showed her some games the boys liked to play with string. And then she watched the brothers wrestle. Shem was clearly bigger and stronger, but Ila could not help feeling impressed with Ham's persistence.

Ham doesn't give up easily, she observed. *Perhaps someday he will even be able to overpower Shem.*

Soon Noah and Naameh came in with baby Japheth.

Noah settled himself on the floor. "My grandfather, Methuselah, lives," he began. "He's helped me to see what we're here to do."

"I fell asleep during our visit," Shem announced. "But guess what... I like berries and so does Grandfather!" He glanced shyly at Ila. "And I told him about you and how we found you."

Ila flushed. That made her happy for some reason.

Noah began telling his story. She had much to learn about him; he confused her sometimes.

"Men are going to be punished for what they've done to this world," Noah was saying now. "There will be terrible destruction—not from fire but from water. But our family has been chosen for a great task. We have been chosen to save the innocent."

"The innocent?" Shem echoed. "What do you mean?"

Ila was glad to see that Ham, and even Shem, were perplexed too.

"The animals," Noah explained.

"Why are they innocent?" Ham wanted to know. "I don't understand."

"Adam and Eve sinned, and they were cast out of Paradise," Ila blurted out. "But the animals live still as they did in the Garden. That's why they are innocent and man is not!"

"Good, Ila!" Noah smiled at her and Ila flushed, happy that she had pleased him and knew something that the boys did not. "We need to save enough of the animals to start again," Noah went on.

"But what of us?" asked Ham. "What will happen to our family?"

"Well..." Noah looked thoughtful for a moment. "I suppose we get to start again too. We get to start again in a new and better world. But first we have to build."

"Build what?" Shem asked.

Ila was curious too.

"Methuselah gave me a seed," Noah explained. "It's from the Garden of Eden." They all hurried after Noah as he stepped outside the tent. He pulled a brown seed from a small pouch in his pocket and then bent down and planted it in the earth.

He turned to face them. "A great flood is coming. The waters of the heavens will meet the waters of the earth," he said gravely. "So we must build a vessel to survive the storm. We must build an ark."

An ark? thought Ila. *An ark to hold all those animals?* It would have to be enormous!

She glanced at Shem, who was grinning at his father's words. She knew why. Part of what Noah was saying, like the violent storm, sounded very frightening. But another part of his story sounded very exciting—like a brand-new adventure.

"You're a traitor!" a voice snarled. "You've been helping them!"

Sometime before dawn, loud voices and sounds woke Ila. She got up from her bedroll and lifted the tent flaps to peek outside. A band of Watchers stood there, arguing.

Noah started yelling as some of them dragged Og away. "Stop!"

The leader of the Watchers, Samyaza, spun around and glared at him.

"There is work to do!" Noah added quickly. "Please help us."

In response, Samyaza stormed over to Noah. Ila felt the earth tremble under his feet. She stepped back a little.

"Help you?" Samyaza repeated. "We tried to help your kind once. We lost *everything* because of you!"

"Not everything," Noah said. "And we can save what is still left. We can serve Him again."

"You treacherous snake!" Samyaza thundered. Ila jumped as he raised an arm to strike Noah.

"No!" she cried, rushing out of the tent.

Samyaza halted. But it wasn't because of Ila, she quickly realized. Instead the Watcher was staring at something, stunned by something in front of her.

By now everyone had awakened and stepped out of the tent.

"How amazing... " Naameh murmured.

Ila looked down. In the spot where Noah had planted Methuselah's tiny seed, water was bursting out of the dry earth. Cracks spilled open at their feet, small rivers starting to push through the dry ground.

Is this the great flood coming? Ila wondered. But Noah had said there would be time to build an ark. It seemed too soon for the great flood to begin...

Soon the earth began to rumble.

Ila grabbed Shem's arm. "What is that noise? Is it an earthquake?"

He just shook his head, looking around. He didn't know what was happening either.

The sound grew louder and louder as the earth shook and boomed. And then suddenly Ila gasped. All around them, green shoots shot up from the earth! They were plants... trees... growing faster than anything she could imagine. By the time the sun rose, Ila could see that the empty, dark landscape was gone. Now a thick forest of tall trees surrounded them.

Ham looked terrified. "What is this, Father?" he asked. "What's going on?"

"This... " Noah smiled broadly and gestured at the tree trunks, "is our Ark!"

Most of the Watchers were gazing at Samyaza, waiting uncertainly to see what their leader would do. At last, the giant leader limped over to one of the tall trees. He touched the trunk, and then stared up at it as if he were in a trance.

When Samyaza turned back to Og, Ila saw tears glistening in his eyes. "We will help this man," he said.

3

TEN YEARS LATER

LAUGHING, ILA RAN THROUGH THE FOREST. SHE RUSHED past the tall leafy trees, ducking under a few low branches.

"No!" she shrieked playfully.

Right behind her was Shem. He quickly caught up to her and grabbed her around the waist.

"No!" she cried again. She giggled as he gently wrestled her to the forest floor.

"No, please, no!"

"Yes!" he said, biting her neck softly.

"Yes..." Ila closed her eyes, inhaling his scent, which had become as familiar to her as the scent of the dense forest where they lived.

The two of them had been friends first, of course, when they were young, but as they grew, it hadn't taken long for their friendship to blossom into something different. Now Ila loved him with a fierceness she hadn't known was in her.

Shem kissed her lips. She put her arms around his neck and kissed him back. Then she stared into his eyes. They were so green, almost the color of the leaves on the trees around them. She thought he was strong and beautiful.

They kissed for a long time. Slowly, his hands and lips glided lower. He lifted her shirt, his hands quickly finding their way inside.

"Shem..." She tried to stop him, but his lips had already found their mark—the thick scar that traveled along her belly. She flushed as he kissed it tenderly.

His hands went lower, as Ila knew they would. "Shem..." she said again, wincing this time. "Please..."

Reluctantly, he lifted his head to look at her. "It still hurts?" he asked softly. "It still hurts when I touch you there?"

"Yes." She nodded, trembling. "It still hurts."

He dropped his head and let out a long sigh.

Ila turned away. They had been through this many times before, and Shem was usually patient. But she could feel his frustration building. And it pained her to know that she was the one causing it.

She used to tell him that things would get better, that she might heal inside, or learn to bear the pain, but she rarely said that anymore. They both knew the truth: Ila's injury had left painful scars and had made her barren. So there was no hope of expanding their family, of having the sons and daughters that they both wanted. Nor was there much hope of Ila's finding pleasure in lying with Shem as a wife.

Can one be happy yet disappointed at once? She wondered.

Snap.

As they lay there in silence, they both heard a branch crack.

Shem leaped to his feet. "Who's there?" he demanded. Ila spotted a flash of color behind some bushes.

Shem saw it too. "Ham!" Shem bellowed, charging at him.

But Ham had a good head start. When Shem returned a minute later, he vowed to pummel his younger brother next time he saw him.

"Ham needs to grow up," Shem snapped. "I'm tired of him spying on us. I told him last time..."

Why is Shem so angry? Ila wondered. Then the answer came to her. *It's my fault. It's because of me.*

"Shem," Ila said gently. "Ham does not have a wife. There's no one here for him. Ham just..."

Ila wanted to say more, but something unusual in the sky made her words trail off.

The sky was filled with a stream of birds—thousands, maybe millions of birds—so many of them, the sun was blotted out as the massive flock flew over the forest.

Shem saw them too. He turned to Ila with a stunned expression.

"Let's go!" she said. She reached for Shem's hand and they took off, running.

In the clearing where the Ark was being built, Noah and Japheth were also watching the sky. As Ila and Shem drew closer, she could see that Noah's face was lit up with joy.

"It begins!" he declared when he saw Ila and Shem. Together they all watched as the birds flew lower, slowly descending toward the boat in the center of the clearing.

Ila let out a breath. It was an amazing sight. Just as Noah had promised, two of every kind of bird imaginable had arrived—raptors, song birds, seabirds, parrots, hundreds of species. Most of them she'd never seen before. The sky was a tornado of colorful beating wings.

"What an incredible sight!" Shem murmured.

He squeezed her hand and she nodded, the earlier tension between them melting away.

Soon Ila rushed into the Ark to prepare for the birds' arrival. She helped Naameh lay dried leaves for bedding as the flood of birds began pouring inside.

By now the Ark was nearly finished, and just as Noah had envisioned, it was an enormous ship with three expansive decks that were all connected by ladders and intricate walkways. All over the ship were spaces designed to hold two of all the animals on earth.

Ila and Naameh finished preparing the nest boxes. The

boxes were stored on the top deck, where the family would have its hearth and living space.

When the nest boxes were ready, the birds seemed to know exactly what to do next. Instinctively, they swarmed to the top of the ship and jammed themselves into the boxes.

Noah had also known exactly what to do, Ila realized with more amazement. He had planned and built the Ark perfectly. Every bit of space built for the birds was now filled.

Later, Ila swept the deck. The boys helped Noah calm the birds by burning some of Naameh's herbs in a brazier. As Noah walked along swinging the brazier, the birds fell instantly to sleep.

Ila glanced at Ham. She wondered if Shem had ever confronted him about his spying on them in the woods. Ila was sad that Ham felt so lonely. She knew Shem was annoyed at him, but she hoped Shem had not been too hard on his younger brother.

Japheth stopped suddenly in front of the doves. They'd been the first birds to land in the clearing, and the young boy seemed enchanted by them. Ila smiled as he reached out now to stroke one.

"Careful, Japheth," Noah warned. "See, that's the boy one and there's the girl. After the storm, they will become parents, and their hatchlings will spread across the world.

"We have to be gentle with the birds," Noah went on.

"And we have to be very protective. If something were to happen, it would be a small piece of Creation lost forever. All of these creatures are now in our care." He touched Japheth's chin. "It's our job to look after them."

Japheth smiled proudly, pleased to have such an important job. But when Ila looked over at Ham, she could see him watching the birds with a different expression. He looked thoughtful and maybe even a bit worried.

Ila suspected she knew what he was thinking—that the birds had mates while he had none.

The two of us have something in common, Ila thought. Like Ila, Ham was worried about the future, sad that he might never have his own family.

She watched him a while longer. *I will find Ham later and try to talk to him,* she decided.

The next animals to arrive at the Ark were not as pretty as the birds.

"Snakes!" Japheth shouted one day as he burst out of the woods and ran into Naameh's arms.

Ila was sitting with Shem. Ham and his father sat nearby at the cooking fire, discussing something in low tones.

"Snakes!" Japheth cried again. "And other reptiles. They're crawling all over the forest floor!"

Ila looked toward the woods and could see them for herself—snakes, lizards, turtles, crocodiles, and more. Above the crawling reptiles were swarms of insects. They were all headed for the Ark.

Naameh lifted her eyebrows and looked at Noah. "Reptiles and insects are coming with us too?"

He smiled at her, amused. "All that creeps, all that crawls, all that slithers."

Ila shivered. She didn't like reptiles much either.

After they had loaded the new arrivals on to the Ark and sealed the hatch, Ila hurried after Ham.

"So what did your father say about getting you a wife?" she asked him with a grin.

He looked at her in surprise. "How did you know that's what I was asking Father?"

"An educated guess."

"Well, he did not say much," Ham replied. "I reminded him that Shem has you, he has Mother, and even the birds have mates. But what of me? And what of Japheth? What is there for us?"

"Yes," Ila agreed with a nod. "It will be lonely for you and Japheth. What was Noah's response?"

"He reminded me of all the Creator has done. How He sent wood for the Ark and sent the animals here too. Father believes that the Creator sends us all we need."

"Did that satisfy you?" Ila asked him.

Ham shrugged. "I will be satisfied when our wives arrive."

Ila smiled again. "Perhaps Noah was talking about patience. If you are patient, the Creator *will* eventually send what you need."

And send it to me too, she thought, remembering the issue that was coming between her and Shem.

4

AS THE DAYS PASSED, ILA AND HER FAMILY ALL CONTINUED working on the Ark, nailing the last boards, tarring the roof, cleaning and preparing the animals' homes.

But Ila felt a new urgency in the air. Their time was running out, and they all knew it. The storm would be here soon.

One day Noah sent Ham and Japheth into the woods to collect kindling. Ila helped Naameh stir hot tar so Shem could lay it on the Ark.

As they worked, Ila noticed Naameh glance toward the woods several times

"Are you worried about the boys?" Ila finally asked her.

Naameh nodded. "They should have returned by now. They have been gone for a long time."

"Perhaps they are playing a game or chasing deer," Ila reassured her. "I'm sure they will return soon."

Soon Ila headed into the woods herself to collect buckets she had hung on trees for sap. Just then Japheth burst through the trees, racing toward the clearing. He was alone.

"Father! Father!" he yelled.

Noah looked up from where he was helping the Watchers stack firewood.

"A huge man came to us in the woods!" Japheth's words tumbled out. "He has battle scars everywhere, and there were warlords and families with him. The man is still talking to Ham. I think he is coming here now!"

Noah held up a hand to make Japheth slow down. Then he made Japheth repeat everything more slowly.

Noah nodded and ordered everyone to stay near the ramp. "Hide there. All of you."

Ila hurried up the ramp behind Shem.

From her vantage point, she could soon see movements along the tree line. Then a band of people—about fifty or more warlords—stepped into the clearing. Behind them were some women and families. As they came closer, she saw that a powerful-looking man gripped Ham's shoulder.

Ila drew in a breath. Japheth was right. The man with Ham looked terrifying. He was huge and muscular, his body covered in battled-dented armor. Scars marked his face, and something about his expression instantly chilled her.

"Who's that?" she whispered to Shem. He just shook

his head, his eyes frozen on the frightening scene unfolding before their eyes.

Ham walked stiffly, looking uneasy, Ila thought, but not exactly afraid. Ham held something in his hand.

Noah stood tall as he faced the man and his band of warlords. "Ham," he said calmly. "Come here."

But the man tightened his grip on Ham, a smile curling along his lips. "Do not take my best soldier."

"He is nothing of yours," Noah retorted.

"Look at his hand on that weapon," the man said. Now Ila could see that Ham was holding an axe. "I believe he *is* something of mine."

"Ham," Noah said forcefully this time.

Ham slowly stepped away from the stranger.

"Leave the weapon there," his father commanded.

"No," Ham said stubbornly. "He gave it to me."

"Do as I tell you!" Noah ordered.

Ham hesitated for another minute and then tossed down the axe. Embarrassed and angry, he stomped past his father, heading toward Ila and the others on the Ark.

As Ham marched away, the stranger turned his gaze to the Ark. "When I heard the talk of miracles, I dismissed it," he remarked. "But then with my own eyes, I saw the massive flock of birds fill the sky. They were flying here, to your Ark. So I had to come."

"There isn't anything for you here," Noah declared.

"Actually..." The warlord gestured around the clearing

with his arms. "This all belongs to me. This land, this forest..." He scoffed as he looked at the Ark. "As well as that stronghold of yours. Did you really think you could protect yourself from me in that ship?"

"The ship is not protection from you."

"Then what is it?"

"An ark," Noah replied. "To hold the innocent when the Creator sends His deluge to wipe the wicked from this world."

"The Creator!" The man scoffed again. "The Creator does not care what happens to this world. Nobody has heard from Him since He marked Cain!"

Ila knew the story of Cain, how he had been one of the twin sons of Adam and Eve. Cain had killed his twin brother, perhaps due to jealousy when the Creator had seemed more pleased with Abel. The murder of Abel had made Cain the world's first murderer. The Creator marked Cain so that others would not exact vengeance.

"We are alone!" the sinister stranger declared. "We are orphaned children, cursed to struggle by the sweat of our brows to survive." The man looked around the clearing again. "Damned if I don't do everything it takes to do just that!"

At those words, Ila saw Noah suddenly snap to attention. *Noah recognizes him!*

"You are Tubal-cain!" Noah burst out. "Descendant of Cain!"

Tubal-cain? Ila thought in surprise. She knew that name from Shem, who had related the story of his father's family many times. Tubal-cain was the vicious leader of the warlords—and the man who had killed Lamech, Noah's father, at the ancient temple!

Noah's face clouded with anger as Tubal-cain peered at him more closely. "We have met?" the warlord leader asked.

Noah shouted to the men gathered behind Tubal-cain. "I am the son of Lamech!"

Tubal-cain fingered an old snakeskin that was wrapped around his shoulders. Ila could see that he was taunting Noah.

"Eight generations descended from Seth," Noah told him. "Return now to your cities of Cain. Know we have all been judged."

Tubal-cain looked surprised at Noah's response. Ila had the feeling that most people simply obeyed the warlord's orders. "I have men at my back and you stand there alone and defy me?"

The barest hint of a smile crossed Noah's face. "I am not alone," he said.

Ila could see that the Watchers had spread themselves out around the Ark, where they were camouflaged to look like large rock formations. Now, at Noah's words, they all stood up.

When Tubal-cain's troops saw the huge creatures, they backed away in panic.

"Do not fear, my people!" Tubal-cain called. "Don't be afraid! Stand!"

He glanced at the Ark again, and then at the forest and the Watchers. His eyes narrowed. "So His minions are here with you," he said thoughtfully. Then he scanned the sky.

"You claim miracles have happened, and soon there will be a deluge?" He looked back at Noah. "Well, perhaps you are right. Perhaps casting us out of Paradise was not enough for the Creator. Perhaps He will return to finish us off. And, if he does..." His eyes drifted back to the Ark. "I will ride out the storm in that ship of yours!"

Noah shook his head. "There is no escape for you and your kind. Your time is done." He spun around.

"The land is dying," Tubal-cain called after him. "The cities are dead. My people follow me, and more will follow them. I am not afraid of miracles, son of Lamech. If you refuse my dozens of people now, I will return with legions!"

Ila and Shem locked eyes. The warlord would return, with more men? A shiver of fear went through her.

Noah ignored the other man's threat and just continued striding toward the Ark. Still, as he approached, Ila could see worry creasing his brow.

Shem and Ila searched the Ark, looking for Ham. Shem was eager to learn more about how Ham had met Tubal-cain.

They found him near the reptiles. His face was still flushed and angry.

Shem stormed up to him. "What were you thinking, Ham? To speak to Father like that! And to take a weapon from that man?"

Ham glared at Shem.

"How do you know him?" Ila asked, trying to defuse the tension building between the brothers.

"I was in the woods,. gathering kindling. Japheth and I saw some girls. It turned out they were with the families of the warlord. I'm sure you're aware," Ham went on bitterly, "Father has done nothing about getting wives for Japheth and me."

"What did that man say to you?" Shem demanded.

"He said he was the king, even though Father says there can be no king in the Creator's garden. Then he gave me the axe and said it was mine, if I wanted it."

Shem shook his head, looking away. "How could you talk to him, Ham? And take an axe, stained with blood from so many men?"

"Why not?" Ham retorted, furious. "You have a wife already, Shem. You have a future. While I... I... Never mind. You don't understand anything about me!" He stormed off, heading deeper into the Ark.

Our future is not as bright as Ham believes, Ila thought with a pang. Still she knew she was lucky to have Shem. "Ham's upset about having no wife," she said softly to Shem. "Surely you can understand that."

"I do understand my brother's loneliness, yes." Shem nodded. "But I cannot understand his actions sometimes. How could he take a weapon from a man like that—an assassin who struck down our grandfather?"

"Ham didn't know the man was Tubal-cain," Ila reminded him.

"True," Shem admitted. "But when he saw the warlords, Ham should have left with Japheth, not lingered in the forest. And he certainly should have obeyed Father and put down the axe immediately."

"Perhaps Ham will come to his senses soon and apologize to Father."

"Perhaps." Shem still sounded angry. "It's plain to see now that Tubal-cain is a danger to Father and to all of us. Ham had better keep his distance."

"He will." Ila reached up to touch Shem's face, trying to coax him out of his anger. She ran her fingers over his eyes and then over his lips. Then she stood on tiptoes to kiss him.

"I love you," she said.

"I love you too." He put his arms around her and pulled her close. They stood there like that for a few minutes.

Everything seems so perfect sometimes, Ila thought. Full and complete. Yet their future did not seem as certain as Ham had implied.

"I've been wondering about something," she said softly.

"Yes?" He pulled back to look at her.

"Do you ever wish you had a different wife? One who could give you children?"

"Ila..." He lifted her chin to make her look at him. "What we have is enough," he said. "We love each other and—"

"You can't deny that you're frustrated, Shem. I've seen plenty of signs of that. And you deserve better than this. You deserve a wife who can give you a son or a daughter. A wife who knows pleasure. No matter what you say to me, Shem, I can see the truth in your eyes."

"Shh..." He hushed her with another kiss. "Please, Ila, let's not talk about it."

Ila stayed quiet, and let the subject drop. But nonetheless it remained on her mind.

I don't want to stand in his way any longer, she thought fiercely. She loved him too much for that.

More days passed, and more animals came. Ila stayed busy with all there was to do. As she worked, she brooded over what to do about Shem. She could see that Ham sometimes brooded too.

One day there was a loud clamor outside the Ark. When Ila peered out, she could see that thousands more animals had arrived.

"It's the mammals!" Ham exclaimed.

They rushed into the clearing to see the vast ocean of animals close up. There were hundreds of amazing, beautiful creatures, many of which Ila had never seen before— rats and pacas and bat-eared foxes scampered around sabre-toothed bears, while wild dogs and great cats rubbed shoulders with gazelles and antelopes. There were oxen, spiked warthogs and giant white kangaroos. Apes swung from the trees, dropping onto the backs of larger animals as elands and hippos walked calmly by. Japheth stood there with Noah, watching them all in amazement.

Naameh filled the brazier with herbs, to welcome these newest arrivals. Then together they guided the beasts toward their new home at the rear of the ship. The fumes from the lighted braziers put all the animals to sleep.

Still full of worried thoughts, Ila passed by Noah's workshop near the great furnace. He sat at a large workbench, hammering and sawing final pieces for the Ark. She paused, watching him work for a moment. She was about to leave when he spotted her.

"Ila!" he greeted her with a warm smile.

"Should I come back later?" she asked.

"No, no," he said. "Please." He waved toward a stool. "Sit with me."

She smiled nervously and sat down. How could she begin?

"I was wondering about those men who brought Ham back... Will they attack us?" she asked.

Noah's expression turned grave. "They will come when the rain comes," he replied.

"And when will the rain come?" she asked.

"Soon."

She hesitated. "What do you think it will be like?"

"I've imagined it," Noah began.

Ila thought of all the dreams that Shem had described for her—his father's dark nightmares of floodwaters, millions drowning, terrible devastation to the earth.

Noah's face clouded. "I'm not sure there are words to describe it, Ila."

"You see the end of everything." said Ila.

"No." Noah shook his head. "What I see is the beginning. The beginning of everything"

At that she felt herself choke up. She felt that she could never have such a new beginning.

"Ila…" Noah came toward her, concerned. "What is it?"

She shook her head, unable to reply.

"Whatever he has done or said, Shem is very fond of you," Noah said softly.

Ila looked at him, surprised he'd known she was upset about Shem. "Did he speak with you?"

"I have eyes," Noah replied. He waited for her to finish.

"I've been thinking." She took a deep breath. "Shem needs a woman. A real woman, not one who is damaged and scarred as I am. He should have a family. And you know that I can't give that to him.

"I'm not going to deny him those things. Even if he wants me to. I won't do it!"

Noah stared at her, taken aback by the fierceness in her voice.

"Besides," she went on, her tone softening. "Why would the Creator want a barren girl—a woman who can't have children—on his ark? It doesn't make any sense. Surely you can see that too."

"Yes…" Noah nodded, closing his eyes and thinking

deeply for a moment. "It's a very good question, Ila," he said at last.

"When we first took you in, I thought you were going to be a burden. And I didn't want to see anyone else ruined by this world. But I was wrong. You were a gift—a precious, precious gift. Please don't forget how precious you are." He leaned forward to hug her.

Ila felt tears threatening to spill. She knew that Noah loved her as a daughter, and she loved him as a father. But his reminder of their bond didn't change anything.

Shem had been her loyal friend and companion, staying close to her ever since the family had come upon her in her devastated camp. She loved him with all her heart, and owed him something more than she felt she could give.

She pulled herself back from Noah and then looked into his eyes.

"I know you will be going to find wives for Ham and Japheth soon," she said softly. "Please find one for Shem too."

5

"WHERE IS FATHER?" HAM ASKED ILA THE NEXT DAY.

Ila shrugged. She hadn't seen Noah since their conversation the night before.

"Mother said he went to get a look at Tubal-cain's camp last night," Shem put in. He looked toward the woods. "He has not returned yet."

"There are many families living in tents near the camp," Ham put in eagerly. "Perhaps Father will come back with wives for Japheth and me!"

"Perhaps." Naameh looked distracted. "I am not sure where he is... I expected him back before daylight."

"I'm sure he'll return soon, Mother," Shem reassured her. They all got busy with chores. Ham and Shem finished laying the roof while Naameh and Ila gathered more food. As she plucked some herbs from Naameh's garden, Ila noticed a Watcher laying out piles of chains.

What are those for? she wondered. Her mind flashed back to the scene with Tubal-cain and his men. Were the Watchers preparing for more trouble? Noah still was not back, and—

Just then someone burst into the clearing.

"Noah?" Naameh called, eyeing him with concern. She rushed toward him and Ila followed. Noah's eyes looked wild and spooked. "What happened?" Naameh wanted to know.

He stormed past her and began barking out orders. "All this should be inside the Ark by now!" He waved a hand at the supplies and scaffolding in front of the Ark. "We need to make haste. The storm is coming."

Make haste? Noah's words sounded ominous. Ila scurried around with Shem, picking things up.

But Ham hurried after his father. "What of our wives?" he demanded. "Where are they?"

Noah whirled around. "Did you hear what I just said, Ham?" He bent down to pick up some logs and then started up the ramp to the Ark.

Ham stopped him. "When are they coming?" he persisted. "When will our wives be here?"

"There will be no wives!" Noah replied.

"What?" Ham was stunned and so was Ila. *No wives at all? No mates for any of the boys?* This didn't make sense.

"Why not?" Ham demanded. "You said the Creator

would give us what we need!"

"Help your brother," Noah murmured. "Now!" He started up the ramp again, but Ham jumped into his path.

Ila held her breath as Ham grabbed Noah's shirt. *How could Noah do this?* she wondered. Ila dreamed constantly of becoming a mother. A mother who would do anything to help her children, and keep her family whole. What had made Shem's father harden his heart? Didn't he realize all the implications of this decision?

"No. Listen to me," Ham went on. "You can't do this. You can't make us leave without wives. How am I supposed to be a man?"

"I said, help your brother!"

Noah pulled away from Ham, but Ham grabbed him again. "You want me to stay a child!"

Noah had clearly heard enough. He reached out and picked up Ham and then tossed him aside.

"I am asking you to be a man by helping your brother. Now do it."

Ignoring his father, Ham dashed off the ramp and toward the woods.

"Ham!" Ila yelled. "Wait!" She started after him. She had just reached the woods when angry voices made her turn around. She saw that Noah was speaking angrily to Naameh as he hacked away at a log with his hatchet.

Naameh stood there, frowning at him as she listened. Then to Ila's surprise, Naameh walked away. She waited until Noah turned his back, and then she tightened her scarf around her head and hurried off.

Where is she going? Ila wondered. But it was not her concern, nor was there time for Ila to linger. She had to find Ham, and find him quickly.

"Ham?" Ila called. She moved deeper into the woods, but there was still no sign of him. She kept thinking of how Noah had looked when he returned from Tubal-cain's camp—spooked and distraught. After all these years of talking about the deluge, it seemed that it was coming at last. The thought terrified Ila.

She kept walking through the forest. "Ham?" Maybe he'd gone toward the refugee camp in search of a wife himself.

She stopped again to listen for his footsteps, but the woods stayed silent.

She walked some more. Finally she entered a clearing. Hunting in the undergrowth was a bent figure. It didn't look like Ham, but... She moved closer. "Ham?"

It was an old, old man with long white wispy hair and a very wrinkled face.

"Don't be afraid, Granddaughter," he said quickly.

"Methuselah? " Ila asked. "Is that you?"

He nodded.

"What are you doing down here?" she asked. She had never known him to leave the mountain before.

"I'm looking for berries," he explained. "I had a craving. Come, help me look for them. My eyes are not as sharp as they once were."

He is acting so strangely, Ila thought. She tried to explain to the old man about Ham.

"Ham ran off. Noah believes that the deluge is coming soon, so I must find Ham."

"There will be time for that," Methuselah assured her. "Come and help me find the berries now."

Not wanting to be impolite, Ila went to help him. She searched the ground, but she didn't see any berries—only dirt and some undergrowth.

Mystified, she turned back to him. "Grandfather, there are no berries here," she said. "Why don't I take you to Noah now?"

"No, no need for that," the old man replied with a strange smile. "You go now. It's time to go."

She stood up uncertainly and then, giving him a wave, started off.

"No, wait," he called after her. "Wait."

Ila turned back to him.

"Ten years you've lived with my own family. Ten years. And you love them. You love Shem."

Ila blushed in response.

"And Noah?" he asked.

"Noah saved my life," Ila replied. "He raised me."

"Yes, he did. And you are now as his own daughter. My

own great-granddaughter. Ten years you have lived in the shadow of my home. And yet, I have never given you my blessing. May I?"

"Yes..." Ila nodded dutifully, but she was still baffled. Why was Grandfather acting so oddly?

He stepped closer, extending his fingers. His ancient fingertips hovered quietly over her belly.

All at once Ila felt something odd within—a sharp, quick sensation that seemed to pierce her belly.

Then, as quickly as it had come, the feeling passed. Ila blinked and looked at Methuselah. His eyes suddenly seemed bright and vivid, and around her, the forest seemed lit up too, thrumming with life. What's happening? she wondered. Somehow she did not feel frightened. Instead she felt calm, at peace.

"Ham? Ila?"

A familiar voice was calling her. "Ila?"

"You can go now," said Methuselah. "Go to him," he urged.

It was Shem. He called her again.

Excited to see him, she ran to him and charged into his arms.

"Ila!" he said, laughing. "I'm happy to see you too. But we have to find Ham and get back to the—"

"Shem..." She cut him off with her kisses. He tried to grab her arm and make her stop, but she held him so tightly, he couldn't get away. She kissed him deeply on the lips and then reached for his shirt and pulled it off.

"Ila..." He groaned. "We have to..." Soon, helpless to stop her, he gave in. Hungrily, he began caressing her face and her throat, and then the scarred skin along her belly.

They dropped to the forest floor, and Ila quickly shed her clothing. He kissed her again, and then moving gently, they joined together as one.

"Oh..." Ila tightened her arms around him. He felt so warm and familiar, yet... something suddenly felt new and different between them. She closed her eyes, leaning into him.

"Ila?"

When she opened her eyes, she saw Shem watching her closely. "Is it... am I hurting you?"

"No," she whispered with a smile. "It's fine, Shem. You're not hurting me at all..."

6

"LOOK AT THE SKY!" SHEM EXCLAIMED.

Ila sat up, dressing quickly. Overhead there was no more blue. The clouds, which had been white and wispy earlier in the day, had turned dark and thick. She watched as they churned ominously, forming into a thick dark blanket overhead.

Splat. A tiny raindrop hit Ila's face.

She looked at Shem. "It's coming," she murmured nervously. More raindrops quickly fell, splattering them.

Shem leaped to his feet and grabbed her hand. "Come on!" Together, they raced through the woods back to the Ark.

In the clearing Ila saw that the Watchers had spread out to make a wide circle around the Ark. The chains she'd seen earlier lay at their feet; they also had weapons now.

Naameh waved at them through the thick sheets of rain. As they drew closer, Ila could see that Noah looked worried.

"Where's Ham?" he demanded.

"We couldn't find him," Ila blurted out. "We looked in the forest, but—"

"Board the Ark now!" Noah cut her off. He started for the woods. "I'll find him myself!"

Ila and Shem nodded, racing up the ramp.

"Daughter?" Naameh suddenly stopped Ila and looked at her closely. "Are you alright?" she asked.

"I'm fine," Ila replied, confused. "Why do you ask?"

"You were gone for a long time," Naameh said quickly. "I was growing worried."

Ila quickly changed into dry clothing and tried to comfort Japheth for a while. The younger boy seemed nervous about the rain and everything that was happening.

Then, worried about Noah and Ham, she went back to the ramp to see what was happening outside.

"Now they are coming!" Naameh said in relief.

Ila saw the father and son rushing toward them in the rain. But Ham seemed to be fighting Noah as Noah yanked him toward the Ark.

"No!" Ham shouted, struggling to get free from his father's grip. "Let me go, Father!"

Ila's heart raced when she noticed something else. Marching behind Noah and Japheth was a massive army— hundreds, maybe thousands, of soldiers holding weapons and covered in armor. Just as he'd threatened, Tubal-cain had returned with his legions!

Ham suddenly wrenched free of Noah.

Noah was shouting at him, but his frantic words were swallowed up by the raging storm. It swirled around them ferociously, winds gusting and rain pelting down like nothing Ila had ever seen.

By now the Watchers had also spotted Tubal-cain's hordes marching toward the clearing. With a loud bellow, Samyaza rose. The other Watchers stood too, roaring, and reaching for the long iron chains that lay on the ground. They pulled the chains tightly, forming a long, unbreakable barrier to keep the army back.

Samyaza raised two arms, ready to strike. In another hand, he held a war hammer.

"Samyaza!" Noah was still yelling frantically. "Where is Ham?"

"He's fine. He got through," Samyaza shouted, gesturing toward the other side of the Watchers' chain.

And Ila could see for herself—Ham was racing toward them and had almost reached the ramp. Behind Noah, Tubal-cain's men were forming a huge protective wedge in front of their leader, to shield him. The ground thundered as the army came closer and closer.

Ila closed her eyes, whispering a silent prayer. Surely the giant Watchers could keep the army back. But there were so many soldiers...

Just then Ham burst onto the ship. Naameh rushed toward him. "Ham! Thank goodness..." She tried to hug him, but he pushed past her, rushing away toward the interior of the Ark.

Ila chased after him, following him to the reptile deck. "I searched for you for hours!" she burst out. "So did Shem. Where were you?"

He stood looking at her, water dripping from his soaked clothing and hair. His face was cold with fury.

"What happened?" she asked softly. "You can tell me."

He shook his head, turning away. Ila could see tears in his eyes. "Ham..." she said gently. "Tell me."

"It was terrible," Ham managed to say finally. "The refugee camp... I..."

Ila waited for him to finish.

He shook his head again. "I just ran and ran, to get away from Father. I was so angry about not having a wife, all I wanted was to get away. I walked for a long time until I heard voices. They were from the refugee camp.

"It was full of people, Ila. You can't believe how many people. And how bad things were. Filthy conditions with people starving and fighting. So much suffering and violence. Suddenly some guards appeared in the crowd, and I tried to get away. But then I fell into a trench." He shuddered, remembering. "It was horrible... it was a mass grave!"

Ila took his hand. "Oh, Ham... how awful."

"I tried to climb out, but it was deep and the dirt was loose.

Then I heard somebody among the corpses. It was a girl."

"She was still alive?"

"Yes." He looked at Ila. "She was still alive but left for dead. It was like..."

"Like me," she finished for him. "Exactly like me."

He nodded. "She was terrified. About my age and filthy. But her face... so beautiful," he whispered.

"She didn't trust me at first, but I gave her some food, and she told me her story. The soldiers had taken her sisters." Ham's face darkened. "Her father tried to stop the men, but they killed him. She pretended to be dead too, and they threw both bodies in the trench. I'm not sure how long she'd been there before I came along."

Ham bit his lip. "Her name is... Her name was Na'el."

Ila listened closely to the rest of the story. When the rain started, Ham knew there wasn't much time left; they had to go. He and Na'el raced through the forest, splashing through puddles and mud. Suddenly Na'el tripped, her leg caught in an animal trap, probably one set by the refugees or Tubal-cain's soldiers.

Ham had rushed to her side.

"In the distance I could hear the army, marching toward us. I tried pulling at the trap as hard as I could but I couldn't get it open. Her leg was badly hurt and I didn't see a way to rescue her.

"By now Tubal-cain's men had almost reached us. I knew it was over. I had found a wife myself, but soon both of us would be killed by Tubal-cain's troops.

"Then I heard someone else crashing through the woods toward us. It was Father!"

"He went to search for you when Shem and I returned without you," Ila explained. "The rain had come, and we didn't know where you were."

"At first I was so relieved to see him, Ila," he went on. "There was Father, in time to rescue us both."

"But what happened?" Ila wanted to know. "You returned alone. Where is she?"

"Father," Ham spat out the word. "Na'el was holding onto me. Father grabbed me and tore me away from her."

"What?" Ila couldn't believe her ears.

Ham went on, his fury rising with each word. "I begged him to save her, and Na'el was begging him too. I tried to fight him, to go back to her. If she was going to be killed, I wanted to die with her.

"But he didn't care about what I wanted or about saving her. He just yanked me away from her and forced me to come back without her."

Ila shook her head, trying to understand. How could Noah—who had saved her own life long ago—have acted like this today? He'd let a young girl die at the hands of Tubal-cain's men? For what reason?

"He thinks he saved me," Ham was saying, "but he didn't. He has doomed me. It's as if I've died."

"Oh Ham," Ila murmured. "I'm so sorry."

He let her hug him again, but then he quickly pulled away from her.

"I'll never forget her, Ila." His face darkened. "And I'll never forgive Father. Not for as long as I live. This cannot be the Creator's will."

Ila hurried back to Shem. He stood at the hatch with his parents, anxiously watching the battle outside.

Ila looked for herself. The Watchers were still holding the chains, doing their best to keep back the swarm of soldiers and people. But Tubal-cain and his hordes were driving relentlessly forward through the pounding rain. As the soldiers marched, warlords fired pipe guns filled with tzohar.

"Advance!" Tubal-cain suddenly called out to his troops. "Now!"

Noah whirled toward Shem. "Protect your mother!" he ordered. "Protect them all!"

Shem nodded and held up his spear. Noah ran out, closing the hatch behind him.

Ila stood near a porthole, clutching Naameh's hand as they both tried to comfort Japheth.

Peering out, Ila saw a blast from a tzohar gun strike Samyaza in the chest. The giant staggered back.

"Oh no..." Ila murmured.

Now she could see Tubal-cain burst through the swarm of soldiers. The massive leader of the warlords was moving swiftly with a pike in his hand, charging toward Samyaza!

Samyaza swung his massive arms, trying to protect himself. But Tubal-cain lunged fast, thrusting his pike in the wound in Samyaza's chest.

"No!" Ila gasped as the giant crumpled to the ground. "No..." Then, to her astonishment, there was a loud crackle, and with a burst of flame, Samyaza exploded.

Stunned, Ila turned to Naameh, who held a hand over her mouth in horror.

Ila looked out again. A single bolt of lightning seemed to rise from Samyaza's body. The bolt hung in the air like a rope of light, almost as if it were connecting earth to Heaven.

"His heavenly form is renewed," Naameh whispered. "He is back where he belongs."

The lightning bolt vanished, and from outside, there were shouts and cries, a deafening roar.

"The Creator brings him home!" someone shouted triumphantly. More Watchers joined his cry.

Ila remembered the story Og had relayed long ago—about how the Watchers had yearned to return to heaven after coming to earth, but the Creator had not heeded their prayers. But now...

"Step back!" Shem yelled suddenly. Ila grabbed Japheth and the three of them backed away from the porthole. A second later several soldiers pried open the main hatch in front of Shem.

"Shem!" Ila screamed.

But Shem was ready for the intruders. Moving fast, he speared one of them. As the man fell back onto the ramp, he pulled Shem out of the Ark with him.

Ila watched in horror as two soldiers were instantly upon him.

In the nick of time, Noah rushed up the ramp, startling Shem's attackers and cutting them down.

"Back inside! *Back inside!*" He thrust Shem into the Ark and then slammed the hatch closed again.

Boom! Outside, explosions rocked the earth and sky. Ila looked back out the porthole, and saw lightning flash in the sky again and again and again. One by one, the Watchers were disappearing.

Tears streamed down her face. Sweet, powerful Og and fierce, brave Samyaza... The Watchers who had been their helpers and protectors for so long.

Shem wrapped an arm around her, his head bent in sorrow too. "They're gone," he whispered. "But they've returned home."

They stood together watching the sky. Outside, the rain and wind pummeled the Ark relentlessly. Noah was still out there... Ila prayed that he was safe.

She turned to Shem. "What of Tubal-cain? Where is he?"

Shem shook his head. "With luck, he's dead," he answered gravely. "I saw no sign of him out there."

* * *

For hours the men and the Watchers battled, and the storm pounded the Ark. Shem ushered them all up to the hearth, saying they would be safer up there. Then he went to look for Ham, whom no one had seen for hours.

Ila huddled there in the darkness with Naameh and Japheth, waiting for the men to return, and for whatever was about to happen next. She tried to contain her fears, doing as her father had told her—filling her mind with things she loved: Shem, memories of the lush green forest where they had lived for the last ten years, Ham and Japheth, friendly Og...

But still her fears seeped in. Noah had described how the water of the heavens would meet the water of the earth. And that was certainly how it sounded now. She pictured huge geysers of water shooting up from the earth as the heavens let loose their own rivers of water.

If Noah were right—if the Creator's message to him had been clear—no one outside the Ark would survive this monstrous storm.

Ila was starting to wonder if anyone *inside* the Ark would survive it either.

Soon they heard loud frantic shouts from outside. Ila and Naameh exchanged glances, but they didn't say anything, not wanting to alarm Japheth. The younger boy was calm at that moment, distracted by a game he was playing with rocks on the floor.

Shem returned with Ham. And then, with a booming force, something slammed into the Ark—a massive wave. Its sound and its force were like nothing Ila had ever known.

Naameh screamed, and grabbed Japheth. Ila struggled to hold on as the huge ark lurched, and then seemed to crest in the huge waves. When the ship settled, the family huddled again in the darkness, waiting for Noah. Naameh whispered prayers as water exploded all around them.

At last the hatch opened and they all looked up.

"Noah!" cried Naameh with relief as he tumbled into the chamber.

Ila looked at him. Blood covered much of his face. What terrified her though was the look in his eyes. He appeared stunned, haunted, overwhelmed by all that he had just witnessed.

7

"PLEASE, NOAH." ILA STOOD IN FRONT OF HIM, PLEADING with him. "People sound desperate. Can you not hear them wailing outside?"

Noah didn't reply to her. Instead, with a chunk of tzohar, he ignited the great furnace. The chamber lit up.

As the fire blazed, Ila paced back and forth in front of the hearth. *This is unbearable*, she thought.

Outside the Ark, floodwaters had covered the land, rising almost to the top of mountain peaks. When she looked through the Ark's portholes, she could see hundreds of survivors clinging to ice-covered rocks, screaming for help.

She had also seen some people trying to swim toward the Ark, but the water was too rough and too cold. None of the swimmers had made it.

She tried to talk to Noah again. "There must be something we can do to help those people. We could drag ropes for them."

"The people cannot all be soldiers from Tubal-cain's army, Father," Shem put in. "They are just people. And there is room aboard our Ark."

Noah sat down, staring forward. Ila could see his stubbornness in the set of his chin and the hardness of his eyes. He would never yield.

Naameh begged him too. "Surely, Noah, we could take a handful of survivors aboard."

"There is no room for them," he said resolutely.

Finally, Ila whirled away from him, angry and upset. How could he show so little mercy? Was this really what the Creator wanted, what He had commanded?

Later, the family ate supper together, sitting on low cushions and rugs. But only Noah and Japheth could eat. Ila and the others left their plates untouched. Since they'd boarded the Ark, Ham had kept his distance from everyone, even Ila. She glanced at him now, worried about his state of mind. He looked brooding and angry and lately she had noticed he was behaving strangely – keeping to himself, staying in the shadows inside the Ark as if he were hiding something.

Noah finally finished his meal and put down his plate. "Soon, everything we knew will be gone," he told the family.

"All that is left of Creation will lie within these walls. And outside, just the waters of chaos again."

He looked directly at Ham, who stared back with a stony expression.

"You're angry," Noah said. "You judge me, Ham, as do the rest of you. Let me tell you a story," he went on. "This is the first story my father ever told me. It is a story that I have told each of you."

He lifted the small tzohar lamp as he began. Ila said nothing, as did the others.

"In the beginning, there was nothing." Noah covered the lamp, plunging the room into darkness to show them.

"Nothing but the silence of infinite darkness. But the breath of the Creator fluttered against the face of the void, whispering, 'Let there be light.'

"And light was. And it was good. The First Day," he went on.

"And the formless light took on substance and shape. A Second Day.

"And our world was born. Our beautiful fragile home. A great warming light nurtured its days. And a lesser light ruled the nights. And there was evening and morning. Another day.

"And the waters of the world gathered together. And in their midst emerged dry land.

"Another day passed. And the ground put forth the growing things. A thick blanket of green, stretching across all Creation. And the waters too teemed with life. Great creatures of the deep that are no more. And vast multitudes of fish some of which may still swim beneath these seas. And soon the sky was streaming with birds.

"And there was evening. And morning. A Fifth Day. Now the whole world was full of living beings. Everything that creeps and crawls. And every beast that walks upon the ground. And it was good."

Ila's eyes were closed as she listened to the familiar story. She didn't want to listen to him somehow, but his words still seeped in. And now, amid all the suffering and terrible destruction she'd seen, the story sounded different to her.

"It was all good," Noah went on. "There was light and air and water and soil. All clean and unspoiled. There were plants and fish, fowl and beast. Each after their kind, all part of the greater whole. All in their place and all was in balance. It was paradise. A jewel in the Creator's palm.

"And then..."

Ila opened her eyes.

"And then the Creator made man. And by man's side, the Creator made woman. He gave us a choice. Follow the temptation of darkness, or hold on to the blessing of light. Our birthright.

"The man and woman ate from the forbidden fruit and their innocence was extinguished. And so for the ten generations since, Adam has walked within us. Brother against brother. Nation against nation. Man against Creation. We murdered each other. We broke the world. We did this.

Man did this. Everything that was beautiful, everything that was good, we shattered."

Ila was thoughtful, remembering the raid upon her family's camp and the violence outside. It was true. Man's violence and destruction was undeniable. But did that justify Noah's own choices? She thought again of Ham's Na'el... the desperate people outside the ship...

"Now it begins again. Air, water, earth, plant, fish, bird, and beast. Paradise returns. But this time, there will be no humans. If we were to re-enter the garden, it would only be to destroy it once more. The Creator has judged us... humankind must end."

Ila sat, speechless.

Shem automatically reached for her hand, squeezing it tightly. She could see Naameh holding Japheth tightly too, tears in her eyes. Only Ham's face stayed cold and stony as Noah went on, explaining to them what was to come.

"Shem and Ila, you will bury me and your mother. Ham, you will bury them. Japheth will lay you to rest. You, Japheth, you will be the last man. And in time, you, too, will return to dust. And creation will be left alone, safe and beautiful."

Ila stared at him, still unable to speak.

Noah looked at Ham. "I'm sorry about that girl," he said softly. "And I'm sorry for you. But we have been entrusted with a task much greater than our own desires."

Ham just glared at his father, too full of fury and shock to say anything. He jumped to his feet and rushed away from the hearth.

With a sigh, Noah sat back. No one said anything.

Ila held Shem's hand. In the silence, she heard only the rain, the endless pounding rain, and the rush of her own thoughts.

Why had Noah given up on the idea of wives for Ham and Japheth? He had obviously never even considered her own request for a fertile wife for Shem. What his children wanted, or needed, had no effect upon him.

And now there was more—larger implications that stretched beyond their own small family.

Did Noah really mean what he had said? Ila wondered. *Was it the end of humankind?*

Somehow the days passed. Ila tried to stay busy. She spent time with Shem, talking and lying together. She played games with Japheth and tried to help Naameh with preparing food and tending to the animals.

Sometimes she made an effort to talk to Ham. But he had retreated so far into himself, he was impossible to reach.

One day while she was sweeping the reptile deck, she thought she heard him talking to someone.

Maybe he's talking to himself, she thought. That would not surprise her since he spent so much time alone and seemed so lonely.

Or more likely, her mind was playing tricks on her. That seemed quite possible too, given the relentless thrumming of the rain and the strangeness of their circumstances.

That night Ila couldn't sleep. She left Shem and walked down to the second deck. As she walked along, she could hear voices rising and falling.

Ila looked up The main hatch was open, and Noah stood staring into the darkness while Naameh stood behind him. Outside it looked like cold sleet was mixing with the rain.

"What happened to you?" Naameh was asking. "What made you change your mind about Ham and his wife, about our future?"

Noah stood silently for a moment. "The refugee camp," he blurted out finally. "The day I went to look at Tubal-cain's camp for myself... I thought perhaps I'd also find wives for Ham and Japheth. Ila wanted me to find a new wife for Shem as well."

"What?" Naameh clapped her hand over her mouth. "But I..." Her words trailed off, and Ila thought she seemed upset by this.

"Ila was thinking of him... She wants him to have a wife who can bear children," Noah explained.

"I saw horrors at the camp, Naameh," he went on. "Tubal-cain is a heartless monster. There were starving refugees trading children for meat... girls shackled to serve soldiers' needs... riots and violence...

"The Creator was speaking to me again, showing me once more the devastation that we have brought. Mankind destroys everything—other humans, the land, the sea. More than ever, I see now that mankind must be punished, washed clean of sin..." Noah kept speaking, murmuring more things to Naameh that Ila could not hear.

Then his voice rose again. "I see no more land. Everything out there must be dead by now."

Naameh reached for his hand and he turned to grasp hers.

She has been his wife for many years now, Ila thought. *She knows him better than anyone.*

Could Naameh make sense of what was happening... of Noah's choices?

"It had to be what He wanted, Naameh. You see that, don't you? It's the Creator's will. I am only..."

Naameh spoke gently. "What I see, Noah, is how hard this was for you to do. As a man who respects life. A man who loves his children. I could not have borne the burden. Not like you."

She took his face in her hands. "You have been strong. But it's done. It is done now. You can put that burden down."

Ila slipped away as a sob escaped from Noah and Naameh comforted him.

For the first time in many days, Ila found her heart softening toward Noah, her adoptive father. She knew it was wrong to eavesdrop on others, but hearing Noah had helped her. She had caught a glimpse of the man she knew. The man who had saved her life, and treated her lovingly as his own daughter.

8

ILA HAD BEEN FEELING SICK. HER STOMACH CHURNED and though she ate little, there was an odd taste in her mouth all the time. Shem thought perhaps she was seasick, but Ila wasn't so sure.

Naameh had noticed. "Here." One day she gave Ila a cup.

"What's this?" Ila asked.

"Spit into it," Naameh said.

Ila obediently spat and Naameh rubbed some of the saliva on to a leaf she'd prepared. White speckles immediately started to appear.

Ila saw Naameh shake her head and then heard her murmur something.

"What is it?" Ila asked. "Am I sick?"

Naameh took a deep breath, turning away for a second. "No," she said. "You're not sick. She turned back to Ila. "You're with child!"

"*What?*" A shiver ran through Ila, and she stared at Naameh in shock.

Naameh repeated her words.

Ila shook her head. "But that's impossible."

Naameh shrugged. "We've all seen miracles, Ila. Perhaps we are seeing another."

Ila sat there, still stunned. Then slowly joy flooded through her. This was everything she had dreamed of for Shem and for her... they'd be parents... they'd have a family of their own...

"It is a miracle!" she declared. "I cannot believe it!"

Naameh was smiling too, but there was something else in her eyes...

"What is it?" Ila asked her.

"It's Noah," Naameh replied. "When he learns the news, he will..." Her words trailed off.

Ila felt a stab of worry too. But she tried to push it aside. "It is his grandchild. Surely he will feel some joy too."

Naameh smiled but didn't say anything. Just then Shem entered the room. Ila threw her arms around him and blurted out the news.

He stared at her in disbelief.

"It's true!" she said. "A baby! We're having a baby."

"Oh, Ila." Shem pulled her closer, burying his head in her hair. He echoed her words. "It's a miracle."

Tears streamed down his cheeks, and hers too.

Naameh looked at Ila and Shem. "We shall tell him together," she announced. "The three of us can go to him and share the news."

Ila paced around the hearth, anxious and excited. *Noah will be pleased by the news,* she told herself. It was not what he had planned, but he loved Shem.

And he loves me too, Ila thought. *He's a kind man, a good man*. She remembered the night she'd heard his sobs. *He has been carrying heavy burdens and is not himself.*

At last Shem stood. "It's time, Ila."

She nodded and they turned toward Noah's workshop. Naameh led the way.

"Father?" Shem began.

Noah looked up, obviously surprised to see the three of them there together. "Yes?" he said.

Shem shot a look at Ila, and she stepped forward.

"Father..." She bowed her head. "We have come to ask for your blessing."

"My blessing?" His eyes narrowed and he looked at Naameh, who quickly looked away. "I don't understand," he said.

Ila took a deep breath. "I am with child," she blurted out.

The room was completely silent for a moment.

"But..." Noah shook his head, frowning. "But that's not

possible, Ila. You're barren. You cannot conceive. You must be mistaken."

"I am not mistaken," Ila said firmly. "We are expecting a child."

Noah's face turned dark with fury. He put down his tools, and stepped closer to her. "How is that possible?" he demanded.

Ila cringed and moved backward.

Naameh quickly stepped in front of her, shielding her. "It was Grandfather," she said quickly. "I climbed the mountain to see him."

"What?" Ila looked at her, stunned.

"Grandfather?" Shem echoed. "What are you talking about, Mother?

"I... I..." Naameh began to explain. "I was broken-hearted when Noah decided there would be no other wives, no more children. So I went up the mountain to ask for Methuselah's help."

Noah went pale. "And Grandfather agreed?" he demanded.

"He said..." Naameh faltered. "He said it was your choice, not mine or his. But he also admitted that he is not sure about many things. Maybe the Creator does want the world destroyed because we have corrupted it and filled it with violence. Or perhaps... Perhaps He has other intentions."

Noah just stared at her, waiting to hear the rest of her story.

"At first Methuselah did not want to help me, but then he agreed." Naameh looked at Noah defiantly. "I told him that

I want my sons to have children! I want them to be happy. I can't bear to think of any of my children dying alone. So at last he agreed."

Ila's heart thudded as she listened. Now she understood. That day she had been in the woods looking for Ham, Grandfather had been looking for berries and then he'd asked to bless her... So Naameh had set this all in motion...

Noah stalked over to Naameh. Ila gasped as he gripped his wife's shoulders fiercely. "How am I to understand this?" he bellowed. "You visited Methuselah—for the purpose of undermining the Creator?"

"Yes." Naameh said, defiantly. "I did it to give our children a future," she shot back. "To give all of humanity a future!"

Ila could see Noah seethe with anger. Sobs filled her throat. She had never seen him so full of rage.

"Have you any idea what you've done?" he thundered at Naameh. "All those lives lost? All those people who died now for nothing! There is blood on my hands. Do you know what I might need to do now?"

Naameh stood in silence.

He let her go and spun back toward his workshop. With a single sweep of his arm, he knocked everything down and it clattered to the floor.

Then he buried his face in his hands for several long minutes.

Ila retreated, huddling in the corner with Shem and Naameh. When she glanced at Noah again, he was looking up through the interior of the Ark as if he were thinking about all he had built, the chambers of animals, the years it had taken.

Tears cascaded down his face. Finally he stomped off, smashing through the hatch door and into the rain.

Ila was sobbing, her stomach clenched in terror. Noah was too angry; she had no idea what he was going to do. What would happen next?

Noah stayed out on the deck for a long time. Ila lay curled up on her bedroll, sobbing as Shem and Naameh sat with her.

Naameh stroked her hair. "Try to get some rest, Ila," she murmured.

"Father will come around," added Shem. "Perhaps once the baby is born, Father will forget his harsh words and give us his blessing."

Ila didn't reply. She could hear the doubt in Shem's voice, which matched all her own doubts.

Shem covered her with a blanket and told her to sleep. In the corner he and Naameh murmured in low tones. She closed her eyes tightly, shutting out their voices.

Long ago Noah and Naameh had found her, enveloped her, and made her part of their family. But now it felt as if their family was fractured, broken like the earth.

Ham had been swallowed up by bitterness.

And Noah... Ila didn't know, didn't understand, his actions, all the burdens upon him.

She buried her face in the blanket. *Could this truly be the Creator's will?* she wondered again. The question had haunted her since they had boarded the Ark. Did the Creator really intend to bring such great destruction and suffering to his people? What if... What if Noah was wrong? What if all this time...?

She closed her eyes, trying to sleep. She dozed for a while and then woke up again.

It's so quiet, she thought. Something had changed... The room was completely silent, completely still.

Then she shot up. "The rain!" she cried. "The rain has stopped! Listen!"

Naameh and Shem were sitting nearby. They listened for a moment. Then the three of them rushed out onto the deck, blinking in the sudden light. The sky and sea had turned from black to gray. For the first day in weeks and weeks, there was light.

Surely this is a sign, thought Ila.

Ham and Japheth rushed out a second later. Ila peered at the far end of the ship, where Noah was kneeling. As he prayed, he stared out at the horizon.

Cautiously, Ila and Shem stepped closer. Now Ila could hear Noah's prayers, the same words again and again. "I will not fail you... I will not fail you. It shall be done."

"Father?" said Shem tentatively.

"The rains have stopped," Ila chimed in. "The Creator smiles on our child!"

Noah turned to them. To Ila's relief, his tears were gone. But the look on his face sent a new chill right through her.

"The rains have stopped because of your child, yes," he said slowly. "But He does not smile."

Noah paused to take a deep breath. "If the child is a boy, it shall replace Japheth as the last man. But if it is a girl..."

Ila felt her heart turn to ice as Noah went on.

"If it is a girl who could mature into a mother, then she must die!"

"Are you mad, Father?" Shem burst out. "You are speaking of my child!"

Noah ignored Shem. His eyes were fastened on Ila.

"Should you bear a girl," he went on, "in the moment of her birth, I will cut her down."

9

ILA SAT DOWN AT THE HEARTH, HOLDING THE SACK SHE was stocking with food, her other hand resting on her swollen belly. She'd just felt something sharp within...

A smile slipped across her face. *The baby will be here soon.*

The months since the rains had stopped had passed slowly, each one seeming to gather more tension and worry.

Sometimes Ila had let herself imagine the child growing in her womb. Perhaps the baby would be a son, strong and fast like Shem with his green eyes and bright smile.

Or she might be a girl, with Ila's dark hair and eyes, and her thoughtful ways. Someday Ila could teach her how to gather berries and build a cooking fire, how to stitch a shirt.

Ila had also tried to fill her mind with love and hope, as her father had taught her, but Noah's threats stalked her, day and night. The nights were especially difficult, with all her dark fears rushing in at once. Over these past months, Ila had missed her birth parents more than ever. How she longed to have them here with her now.

The pain had subsided. Ila stood up to finish her task. Then, carrying the sack full of food, she stepped outside. Together she and Shem and Naameh had been making plans. Shem had built a raft from logs scavenged from the Ark.

It sat waiting now at the edge of the ramp, held in place by two ropes.

Naameh and Japheth stood near the ramp.

Ila knew that Naameh never stopped worrying either. Every day Naameh sent out one of the birds from the Ark, hoping it would return with some sign of land, a place to which they could escape. But day after day, the birds came back with no evidence of anything except the endless sea.

Ila looked questioningly at Naameh, who shook her head no. "Nothing," she said softly.

Ila handed the food to Shem. He was lashing down barrels of fresh water.

"We have to go," Ila told Naameh. "We cannot wait much longer."

"Ila…" Naameh ran a hand over her head, distressed. "There is nothing out there, no land anywhere. You have food, water for how long? Weeks? A month?"

"One month," Shem replied. "We can survive."

Naameh tightened her lips. "The raft is small, and the sea could grow rough. Please wait. Please wait until a bird comes back with something. Japheth, send the raven again to search."

Japheth groaned. "He's too tired, Mother."

"Then wake another bird!" commanded Naameh. She forced some dried herbs into his hands. "Get one that can find us a home!"

Ila looked around the deck. "Where's Ham?"

Shem shrugged. "He's off by himself somewhere, as always."

Ila hoped Ham would join them soon, at least for a short time. She missed him, and their time together was precious now.

Just then Noah emerged from inside the ship. Ila saw him watching them. He had seen the raft, he knew their plans. Ila stared back, keeping a protective hand on her belly. His eyes were dark and hard to read.

"No," she said abruptly. "We cannot wait, Naameh. The baby is coming. We must leave today."

She lifted her eyes back to Noah. For a moment he met her gaze. Ila did not flinch or look away. Finally, he did, turning around and disappearing back inside the Ark.

* * *

Working fast, Ila helped Shem finish loading the raft. They tied their bundles of food and some spare clothing under a tarp. Then they gathered a few more things.

When they were finished, Ila turned to Naameh. It was time to say goodbye.

Tears streamed from Naameh's eyes. "Take care of that baby," she managed to say.

Ila hugged her. "I will."

Shem tried to smile. "Do not be afraid, Mother," he said. "We will see each other in the new world."

Suddenly Japheth spoke. His eyes were on something behind them. "Father?"

Ila spun around. Noah stood above them on the roof of the Ark.

Shem pulled her toward him protectively.

Noah looked at Naameh, who glared at him. Then he tossed a bag onto the raft below. Ila screamed as the raft burst into flames. Tzohar? Had Noah thrown tzohar?

Shem was watching the raft burn in horror. "No!" he cried.

Noah leaped down from the roof, landing on the ramp. He reached down with his knife and sliced through the restraining ropes on the raft.

Shem looked distraught. "I thought you were good. I thought that was why the Creator chose you, Father!"

Noah shook his head. "You have it wrong, son. He chose me because he knew I would complete the task. Nothing more!"

Ila stood next to Naameh, who was watching in disbelief.

Dimly, Ila knew Naameh was saying something. But an odd sensation was distracting her. She gasped as she realized that water was trickling down her leg.

She cried out, and Naameh saw what was happening. "It's your time, Ila," she said urgently. "Come with me!"

Shem and Naameh began leading Ila back to the hearth. As she walked between them, Ila couldn't help taking a final look back at Noah. He stood alone. Behind him the raft that Shem had built for their escape was burning and crumbling, flaming bits of debris falling into the sea.

Inside Naameh and Noah's tent, Naameh covered Ila with a blanket. Then Naameh felt Ila's belly.

"You'll be all right, daughter."

"Please keep the baby inside," Ila pleaded with her. "Where it's safe. Don't let Noah—"

Naameh put a finger on Ila's lips. "Your baby is coming," she said. "Don't think about anything else."

Ila winced as another strong contraction came. She closed her eyes, riding the waves of pain as they came and went. *Please let my baby be safe. Please let my baby be safe.*

Shem stood guard outside the tent holding his spear.

More contractions gripped Ila. Naameh squeezed her hand as she called out in pain.

Hours passed. When the pains came, Ila kept her eyes on Naameh's face as Shem's mother gently whispered encouragingly to her. She thought of Shem and her birth parents and Ham and Japheth, all the people she loved. Even Noah. But she couldn't let herself think about the baby right now... she was too afraid, too worried about Noah's terrible threats, and what he would do.

From outside the tent, the women heard roars and a loud bang. Naameh shot a worried look at the tent entrance and then looked back at Ila.

"You are doing well, daughter. It won't be long now."

A new pain tore through Ila and she let out a moan. Another contraction came, and another.

"Now, Ila!" said Naameh suddenly. "Push!"

Ila obeyed. As the contractions came, Ila pushed again and again until...

A loud cry filled the air. At the sound, Shem rushed into the tent. He looked at his mother. She quickly wrapped the baby in a blanket and placed it in a basket on the floor.

"Boy or girl?" he demanded. "Which one?"

Ila watched Naameh's face. She wanted to know too. Naameh didn't answer him right away.

What's wrong? thought Ila. *Why isn't she...?* Suddenly Ila felt more pains. "Naameh," she began. "I..."

"What's happening?" Shem asked in a panic. "What's going on?"

Ila couldn't speak.

Naameh's face had turned white. "There's another one coming," she said.

"What?" said Shem. "Two babies?"

"Yes, twins!" Naameh said. "Two babies, my son! She turned back to Ila. "Push, Ila."

Ila obeyed, pushing again. Soon another child emerged and cried its first breath.

Shem glanced at his mother who was holding the second baby. "Well...?"

Ila was holding her breath. She kept her eyes on Naameh's face, waiting for the answer.

Naameh looked at the infants, and then Ila saw her face fall.

A scream had gathered in Ila's throat even before Naameh spoke.

"I'm sorry. I'm so sorry," Naameh murmured. "The babies are sisters."

"No!" Ila screamed. "No!"

Shem moved to Ila's side and grabbed her hands. He kissed her tears and took a long, deep breath.

"Where's Noah? Where's Noah?" Ila demanded again and again. "Keep him away! Keep him away from our daughters!"

"He will not touch them," Shem said fiercely. "I will make sure of that."

A new fear gripped Ila as she saw Shem pick up his spear again. "Shem!" she cried.

But it was too late. Shem was already racing through the Ark to find his father.

* * *

Ila sobbed and the babies wailed. Somehow Naameh had managed to stay calm. "You must nurse them now," she told Ila.

Ila nodded, and Naameh helped her to lift the babies to her breasts. Her mind was racing.

What was happening between Shem and his father? Could Noah be stopped without anyone being harmed? How could they protect their babies?

From far away she heard yells and loud bangs. She and Naameh exchanged worried looks. Japheth was with Naameh now, but neither of them had seen Ham for some time.

Suddenly, there was a loud scraping sound and the huge ark lurched violently. As the ship bounced and tilted, Ila held her daughters tightly. The sound of wood splintering filled the air.

Naameh gasped and rushed to look outside. "The Ark struck land!" she cried. She took a baby from Ila and bundled her up tightly. She did the same with the other infant. "We must find a safe spot for you now, daughter. A safe spot for all of you."

Ila carried one baby while Naameh held the other as they made their way to the roof of the Ark.

"Stay here, and don't move until I return," Naameh

ordered. "I will see what is happening with the men and come back to let you know."

Ila nodded, too frightened and exhausted to think for herself at the moment. She clutched the babies to her chest, praying softly. *Let us be safe. Let us be safe...*

A brisk sea breeze stirred the air. Ila shivered, though she couldn't tell if it was from exhaustion or the cold. Maybe it was both.

She gazed down at the babies, overcome with love. They were beautiful, tiny fists and dark eyes... Each had a patch of light hair.

What a miracle, she thought, rocking them gently. She wished Shem were here with her now. Worries rippled through her. Was he safe? Would he harm Noah?

Ila wasn't sure how much time had passed when a shout rose from below.

"It's a boy!"

That's Naameh, Ila realized. And then she heard Noah's voice.

"Move away," he ordered. Then there were his footsteps.

"Where is she?" he demanded.

One of the babies squirmed in Ila's arms. "Hush, little one," she murmured. "Please don't cry." Desperately, she tried to soothe her. Then the other baby woke up and began to cry.

No... no... Ila thought in desperation. Frantic, she was about to try to nurse them.

But then another shout came from below.

"No!" Naameh moaned. "No, Noah! You can't touch them. They are beautiful!"

"*They?*" Noah echoed. "Are you telling me there are two?"

"You can't kill them!" Naameh pleaded with him. "You can't!"

Now Ila could hear his steps. He was coming up the ladder, coming closer and closer to her and her infants with every step.

Ila's heart pounded in her chest, her prayers replaying again and again as she sobbed. *Please keep us safe. Please keep us safe.*

Around her the wind picked up, and suddenly she thought of Methuselah and his blessing that day in the forest.

What had Noah once said to her...? It was the day she'd asked him about a wife for Ham. He'd said that she was a precious gift. Ila looked at her daughters. Would not he see these babies, too, as a precious gift?

All at once the air grew still. Ila closed her eyes, feeling her heart slow too. She breathed slowly, in and out, in and out, crying still but paying no attention to the sounds behind her, Noah limping toward her.

In her arms, the babies were still crying. *Are they hungry?* she wondered. Or could they could sense all the madness and violence around them?

At last he reached her.

Ila spoke softly. "Noah, please. These are my children. Your grandchildren."

"I will not be stopped."

Ila turned to look at him. His clothes were torn, and he was wounded, bruised, and bloodied by whatever had happened below with Shem.

Where is Shem? she wondered again. *And Ham...?*

Gazing at his face, the steely look in his eyes, Ila knew it was hopeless. She took another deep breath to collect herself and swallow her tears. "I know I cannot stop you, Noah. But my babies are crying."

She swallowed hard. "Please don't let them die crying. Please let me calm them. Please just... Just let them be at peace."

He stared at her, saying nothing for a long time. And then finally he nodded.

"Thank you," Ila whispered. She started to hum. It was a lullaby she loved, a lullaby filled with tender memories of the man who had found her and taken her into his arms like a father one night long ago.

> *The moon is high*
> *The trees entwined*
> *Your father waits for thee.*
> *To wrap you in his sheltering wings*
> *And whisper you to sleep.*
> *To wrap you in his welcome arms*
> *Until the night sky breaks*
> *Your father is*

The healing wind that whispers
You to sleep
That whispers as you sleep.

As Ila sang, her infants hushed. Calm, at peace, they stared up at her.

"I love you," she murmured, caressing each baby's perfect face. Silent tears streamed from her eyes.

At last Ila stood up and turned toward Noah. He reached for the babies, but Ila shook her head. "No."

Noah blinked in surprise. "You do not need to see this, Ila."

"No. I won't hand them over. I will hold them," she declared. *I am their mother*, she thought.

Noah closed his eyes for a moment. Then he tightly gripped his knife. Behind them Ila could hear Naameh, maybe others on the roof now. But she kept her eyes pinned to Noah's face.

"Do it quickly!" she urged him.

In his hand the knife blade glinted in the light. The babies both looked up at him, squinting and blinking.

Tears filled his eyes.

Beside him, Ila could feel something in him melt.

Then he turned from her, unable to look at her or the babies anymore.

Numbly, she watched him stumble to the edge of the Ark. He teetered there, as if he were about to fall or jump.

Slowly, his eyes lifted up toward the heavens and the

Creator. "I cannot do this." His hand relaxed, and the knife plunged into the churning waters below.

Ila heard footsteps behind her. "Shem!" she cried in joy. He scooped up his daughters. Ila hugged him, feeling the two babies' tiny bodies between them.

My husband. My children.

Japheth and Naameh rushed over too. There was no sign of Ham.

"Is Ham safe?" she asked Shem. He nodded. "I will explain everything later."

Ila saw Noah stumble off, heading back down the ladder.

Just then her eyes landed on something in the sky.

It's a dove! she realized in amazement. The white bird was flying toward the Ark, an olive branch in its beak.

10

SIX MONTHS LATER

AT THE HEARTH ILA HELPED NAAMEH AND JAPHETH stack wood for their cooking fire. Tonight there would be fish for supper, and Ila thought she'd easily be able to find some more grapes or berries as well. The floodwaters had receded months ago, and already this island showed plenty of signs of new life—vines hanging heavy with fruit, young saplings sprouting up from the earth, and colorful wildflowers all around them. Birds nested in the trees and all manner of animals were grazing on the hillsides.

Ila looked up and noticed Ham up on the hillside, gazing down at them from near where the Ark had come to rest.

The grounded ship sat behind their camp on the hillside now, worn and decayed from its time at sea.

Shem had caught sight of Ham too and suddenly called, "Japheth!" He and Japheth hurried up to the cliff that overlooked the sea, towards their brother.

I wonder what is happening, Ila thought. But there was no more time to wonder because her daughters were already awake from their nap and crying to be picked up and fed.

She went into a tent to get them from their cradle, smiling at their sweet, still sleepy faces. Then she carried them outside, noticing how much progress Shem had already made on their home. It was a tall, sturdy-looking structure, constructed mainly from boards from the Ark.

Ila fed her babies, the sun warm on her face. *Each day it is easier*, she thought. Each day she was able to release another terrible memory, and put the past a bit further behind them.

But some of those memories would never be released, she knew. They were embedded in her family's story now, like a thread woven inextricably through a garment.

Over time, once she had recovered from the events, Shem and Ham had told her most of what had happened on the day of their daughters' birth.

According to Shem, Tubal-cain had managed to board the Ark during his troops' battle with the Watchers. He was wounded badly, but Ham had found him and bandaged his wounds and brought him nourishment.

"Tubal-cain and I... we had a strange bond," Ham had

said. "From the first time we met. I thought I wanted a way to seek revenge on Father."

The two of them had waited for the right opportunity. Finally, on the day of Ila's labor, Tubal-cain had instructed Ham to lure Noah to the mammal deck. He gave Ham a small knife and told him to wait.

Tubal-cain and Noah battled. And then the Ark had smashed into land, ripping a hole in the hull.

Shem had been determined to stop Noah, too, before he could hurt the babies. Not realizing what was happening between Noah and Tubal-cain, he'd brought down his spear on Noah's head. But then Tubal-cain had come out of nowhere.

"He's mine," Tubal-cain had snarled, desperate to reach Noah first. He tossed Shem aside like a sack of grain.

Shem crashed hard into a beam, and Ham, who was hiding, saw his brother go down.

Tubal-cain raised a rock over Noah's head. "The Ark, the beasts, and all of your women are now mine," he declared. "I will build a new world. In my image!"

But before Tubal-cain could strike Noah, Ham attacked the warlord with the knife.

Ham had turned to Noah then. "Her name was Na'el," he'd informed his father. "She was innocent! She was good!"

The story still filled Ila with grief. She never could have imagined how much her family would change, how violence and sorrow and blame would wrench them apart.

Ila put the babies down on the blanket. Shading her eyes,

she looked up at a cave carved out of the sea cliff. She could see Shem and Japheth enter the cave while Ham hung back, staying near the entrance. She saw him drop a small satchel near the cave opening, and then he turned and left.

Above she could see, too, traces of Noah's solitary life there—the remains of a cooking fire, a basin to collect rainwater, his battered winepress.

She knew that they had gone to find their father. He would be in the same place he spent every day—on the floor of the cave, drunk and ruined.

"Ila?"

Ila was washing a cup in the small stream they used for drinking water when Ham came toward her. Her heart sank when she saw that he was dressed for travel, a bag over his shoulder.

She stood as he approached.

"Ham..." she murmured. She wanted to say more, but there were really no words left. He'd been a fine brother to her.

He smiled sadly at her. "For what it is worth, sister, I'm glad it begins again with you. Maybe we will learn to be kind."

He murmured goodbye and then moved past her.

Ila watched him go, sadness filling her heart.

He had to leave, she knew that. He had to make his own way. He'd never forgive Noah for what had happened to his Na'el, and the bitterness was destroying him.

She glanced up at the seaside cliff again.

It was time.

She finished washing the cup and then started up to the cliff.

Ila waited for him, sitting on a rock looking out at the sea. At last he emerged. To Ila's surprise, his clothes and face were clean. For a moment they stared out at the sea together.

"Ham's gone," Ila told him.

Noah nodded. He seemed to know that already.

"Will he come back?" she asked.

Noah shrugged. "Some things cannot be unbroken."

Ila drew in a breath. "I have to know," she began. "Why did you spare them?"

Noah closed his eyes, looking pained. "I gazed down at those girls, and all I had in my heart was love."

"Then why are you alone, Noah?" Ila demanded. "Why have you shut yourself off and done this to yourself? I can see that you are in anguish."

"Because I failed Him," Noah replied. "And I failed all of you."

Ila shook her head. "*Did* you fail?" she asked. "I believe He chose you for a reason, Noah. He showed you the wickedness of man and knew you would not look away. But when you looked, you saw goodness too. The choice was put in your hands because He put it there. He asked you to decide if we were worth saving. And you chose mercy. You chose love."

Noah looked at her, surprised.

Ila took his hand and held it for a moment. Then she went back to the hearth, where Shem and her daughters waited.

More days passed. Each day Ila looked up at the cliffside, waiting.

Then one day, she took a bucket to collect some berries. Nearby, Naameh was chopping the dirt with a spade.

"I'm planting a new herb garden," she said.

Soon they both heard footsteps. Ila looked up—it was Noah. He had come to join Naameh.

Naameh dropped down, kneeling in the dirt to pull out stones and other debris.

Silently, Noah dropped down beside her. Together they worked, picking the stones out of the family's garden. Neither said a word. But Ila saw their fingers touch and then they embraced.

The wind blew as Ila gathered her family at the top of the mountain. Noah stood with them.

He looks older, she realized. The years and events aboard the Ark had scarred him, just as they had scarred all of them. Something fierce and determined still lurked around his dark eyes. But something else was present there now too...

Warmth, Ila decided. *Maybe even peace.*

She watched him look at each member of their family: Naameh, Japheth, Shem, his two granddaughters, and then Ila. When he was ready, he opened the satchel Ham had left in the cave, uncoiled the ancient snakeskin from its pouch and began the blessing.

"The Creator made Adam in his image and placed the world in his care. That birthright was passed down to us... to my father, Lamech. Then to me and my sons, Shem, Japheth, and... Ham."

Noah slowly wrapped the holy talisman around his arm. Ila saw it shimmer and spread, just as Noah had described to Ila long ago.

He looked down again at the babies in her arms. "And that birthright is now passed to you, our grandchildren. This will be your work, and your responsibility."

Ila watched as the sacred object undulated with a heavenly light. Noah reached out his hand and let the reptile skin tickle the babies' foreheads.

Ila smiled, watching the babies, and then she smiled at Shem. Her arms too full of babies to reach for his hand, she stepped closer, letting her shoulder brush his.

"We are in another garden, a new Eden," he murmured. And she nodded.

Although some things remain unchanged, she thought. Once, long ago, Shem's mother had promised that Shem would take her hand and he wouldn't let it go. As he stood beside her now, it seemed to Ila that he was still holding her hand, and always would be.

Noah's next words seemed to echo from the top of the mountain. "So I say to you. Be fruitful and multiply, and replenish the world!"

Ila bowed her head in gratitude. Silently, she thanked the Creator for Shem and her daughters and the rest of her family gathered around her. For Ham, who might be making his way across new territory, where he'd find a new beginning. And for Noah and the choice he had made, the peace he had found.

Happiness washed over her.

The storm is finally over, she thought. She could feel the proof of it in her heart. And when she looked up, she saw it above her too. A golden shimmering light filled the sky, forming an arc that suddenly blazed with brilliant colors.

A dazzling rainbow over the earth, and Ila knew it was the Creator's blessing.

THE END

ABOUT THE AUTHOR

SUSAN KORMAN IS THE AUTHOR OF OVER THIRTY BOOKS ranging from picture books and licensed works to YA novels. She has written tie-in novels for *Ice Age*, *Monsters Vs Aliens*, *Kung Fu Panda*, *Kicking and Screaming* and various *Transformers* movies. She has also written YA titles under her own name including *Overexposed* and *Bad Deal* (a 2012 ALA Quick Pick for Reluctant Readers).

susankorman.net